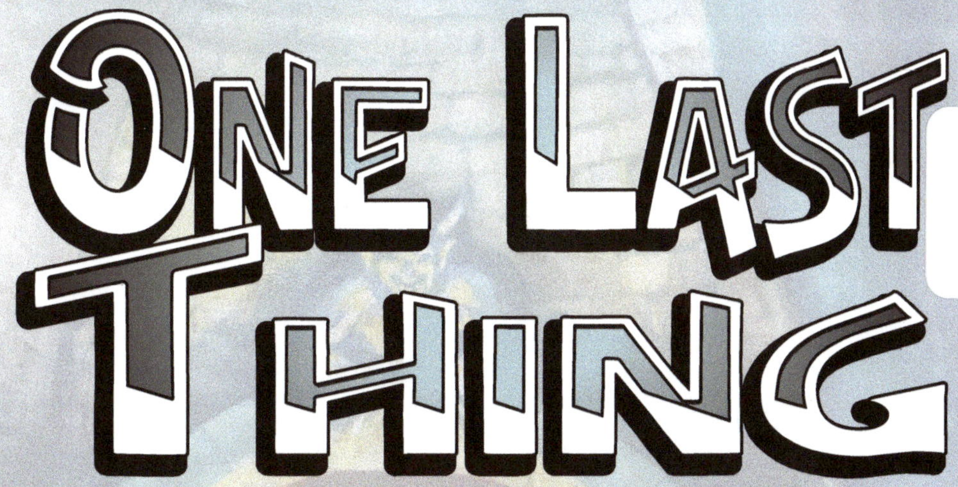

Author:

Casey Christofferson

Editor:

Jeff Harkness

Layout:

Suzy Moseby

Art Director:

Casey Christofferson

Front Cover Art:

Brian LeBlanc

Cover Design:

Jim Wampler

Interior Art:

Adrian Landeros

Cartography:

Robert Altbauer

Project Manager:

Casey Christofferson

Fifth Edition Conversion:

Edwin Nagy

Frog God Games is:

Bill Webb, Matt Finch, Zach Glazar, Charles A. Wright, Edwin Nagy, Mike Badolato, and John Barnhouse

ADVENTURES
WORTH
WINNING

FROG GOD GAMES
ISBN: 978-1-6656-0015-6
5e PoD

Table of Contents

One Last Thing

By Casey Christofferson

A 5e adventure designed for 4 to 6 Tier 2 characters

One Last Thing is an adventure for 4–6 Tier 2 characters, though elements of the adventure locations described here may be suitable for much higher-level play.

The adventure begins in a town, city, castle, or somewhere familiar to the characters where they know various NPC friends they have met along the way. The adventure assumes familiarity with a large town or city and nearby graveyard where the Necropolis of Ankev can be accessed.

Background

A friend has passed to the great beyond. Drinks and libations have been had at his wake and a funeral has lain him to his final rest. Something, however, seems hollow and different about the affair. There is unfinished business, and everyone knows it — yet nobody knows just what it is that everyone seems to have forgotten. Days and weeks stretch by, and things seem to remind you of the loss. It feels almost that the dearly departed has some other task, some incomplete goal that must be achieved before it can move on. Something damning has trapped them in the Underworld and only through the deeds of their closest friends may a final and lasting rest be achieved.

One Last Thing is a haunting trek into the Underworld of the freshly dead to find the one last thing that a dead friend needs to rest in peace once and for all. Through the course of the adventure, characters encounter a variety of challenges involving roleplaying, exploration, investigation, and extra-dimensional travel.

Adventure Summary

This adventure requires a little more groundwork to set things up. First off, it requires the characters to know and trust an NPC who is familiar with their career and exploits. For the purposes of the adventure, this NPC is called "Jaego," but you can and should substitute any NPC who fits the needs of the scenario. As the adventure begins, the characters learn that "Jaego" is dead.

A short time after his death, Jaego begins haunting the characters. First silently, and then with greater amounts of fear-inducing interactions, Jaego leaves clues behind for the characters to figure out exactly what it is that he wants. As the characters pursue the clues that Jaego leaves behind, they eventually wind up at Jaego's gravesite then travel from there to the very outskirts of the Underworld itself where they are led to the fabled Necropolis of Ankev.

The character must carefully navigate the necropolis lest they wear out their welcome in that deathly realm. After exploring the necropolis, the characters eventually come face to face with their friend and discover what Jaego needs to achieve his final rest.

Who is Jaego?

Establishing Jaego as a friend or ally of the characters is a fairly easy endeavor and could be drawn out over 3–6 gaming sessions. For the purposes of the adventure, Jaego serves as a stand-in murder victim who is familiar to the characters. His body was discovered too late to be raised from the dead, and his finances were such that a purchase of such a *raise dead* or *resurrection* spell was impossible as the grim reaper had already laid claim to his soul. The time is short before his soul is traded to Orcus, as so many unclaimed spirits are. It is well known that once a soul is in the custody of the Demon Lord of the Dead, it is doomed forever as a minion of evil.

In life, Jaego was a young bard who never had a hit until he overheard the characters discuss their exploits in a tavern after one of their first adventures. He penned a song in their honor that became popular locally and brought some fame to the characters. Jaego has casually followed the characters ever since. He has been friendly but kept his distance. The characters know him from the fame he heaped upon their name, and the meals and drinks he has quietly but politely plied them with to get their stories. He could be the guy whom they find trapped in the hobgoblin's cell, or he could happen across the characters near the end of a fight, just in time to offer them a boost of inspiration and a bit of healing. Aside from that, he shouldn't be the star of any show before his death. Instead, Jaego is very much the "Hey, do you all remember that guy that is always hanging out?" sort of fellow. In other words, Jaego is a friendly face in the background whom everyone really liked but that nobody can really claim to have known all that well.

So why is Jaego dead? The characters are not Jaego's only topic of interest. Among other things, Jaego was a spy and one-time herald for the court of Count Mercier of Reme, a noble with connections to one of the royal families. Recently, Jaego came into possession of a diary that had some very significant information relating to the rise and fall of regional powers. Jaego was unsure what to do with the information and wanted to share it with the only heroes he knew. Jaego hid the information but was killed by a faction searching for the diary before he could share its secrets with the characters.

Jaego's spirit now seeks to share the location of his secret diary with the characters so that they may decide what best to do with it. The only way for him to tell the characters where he has hidden the diary is by inviting them to visit his restless spirit in the Necropolis of Ankev on the shores of the River Styx!

One Last Thing
1 square = 100 ft.
Etherial Border

Part 1: Jaego is Dead

The adventure begins upon the character's arrival to a familiar settlement such as a town, city, or village that they frequent as a home base or headquarters. They are greeted with news from a familiar barkeep or inn owner that their old friend has been murdered while they were away adventuring. The body was discovered in the basement of an abandoned structure in the foreign quarter, a few blocks from a gambling house he was known to frequent. The victim's body was beyond the help of local clerics and was thus rapidly and summarily buried in a simple plot in the local cemetery due to the onset of putrefaction. Investigators and priests spent some time with the body attempting to use magic and other means to determine the identity of the killer. The constables' report indicated that he had been stabbed multiple times and that his heart had been cut out of his body.

Preliminary Investigations

Characters may speak with local temples or authorities but are given much the same information. It is believed that Jaego went to the gaming house to meet someone and that the person or persons he was intent upon meeting never arrived. He left and was next found several days later, dead and mutilated.

The gaming-house: The Game Master may substitute any gaming house in their campaign world or use one from the Lost Lands such as the famous Fortune's Fool casino in Bard's Gate.

Characters who research deeply into Jaego's past find a lot of dead-ends. An successful DC 20 Intelligence (Investigation or History) check or some legend lore magical ability reveals that Jaego was once in the employ of Count Mercier of Reme. Further investigation of Count Mercier reveals that he has direct familial ties to royalty and has a long-standing rivalry with Earl Brodchek.

Additional research discovers that both nobles live some distance from the characters' current location and any attempts to look up their emissaries in the city results only in information related to shipping, trade, and business investments involving other local nobles and merchants.

Note: Gathering this level of information should involve extremely outside chances on the part of the characters, at least initially, and you may use as much or as little of this information as you deem necessary to further characters into their exploration of the Necropolis of Ankev so they may discover what their friend's last wish happens to be!

The First Haunting

The first haunting affects each of the characters individually. They may be walking about town on other business. For example, the rogue may be busy picking pockets or running a scam. The fighting types may be shopping for armor polish or training in a local warriors' gymnasium. The wizard may be at a library in their local guildhall exploring arcane secrets. Each is visited with a vision of Jaego. At first, they catch a glimpse out of the corner of their eye or hear the bars of the song that Jaego penned in their honor. When the characters turn to look more closely, the image appears fleeting or disappears completely. They must make a DC 15 Wisdom saving throw or become unnerved by the sensation and attempt to flee the area.

A short time later, Jaego appears as a full apparition before the character(s). He is either sitting near them, or walks up to them, and attempts to speak, though the words cannot be heard. His body is translucent and leaks ectoplasm from the various stab wounds that took his life. Just as he begins to communicate, he dissolves with an anguished look on his face.

Characters may be confused by what has happened. In his place are a few pieces of parchment that the characters may recognize from Jaego's moleskin notebook. Upon the page are several notes from a funerary dirge. The song is called "*City of the Dead.*" The song is a lament describing lost souls trapped on the edge of the River Styx where they wait to be taken to the next stop in the afterlife or where Orcus collects them for unending torment in the eternal Abyss.

Characters who research the song in a temple or bard's academy discover that the "*City of the Dead*" is a reference to the fabled Necropolis of Ankev, a waypoint along the River Styx that was once managed by the fabled arch-lich before he parted ways with Orcus, Demon Lord of the Undead.

The Second Haunting

The characters are frightened by a nightmare. In their vision, they see themselves on the street. Suddenly, masked enemies surround them. They hear their words "It's the end for you …" but the name is muffled. Their flesh is pierced with knives from multiple directions. Pain wracks their body, and they lie in the gravel of an alleyway gasping and bleeding in the street. One of the crimson-masked figures approaches with a long, thin blade. The character feels a heavy pounding in his or her chest as the figure approaches. Then everything goes red.

When they are aware again, the character notes that Jaego is walking next to them. He is trying to say something, as if imploring them to listen. Finally, Jaego steps in front of them with a concerned look on his gaunt face, his glazed eyes imploring the characters. He points to himself and then at the archway of the city graveyard before he vanishes with an anguished gurgle.

As the characters awake, they are denied any benefit of rest. No spells are refreshed nor are any hit points recovered from their sleep.

As they awaken, they hear notes from the "*City of the Dead*" playing in their ears as if sung by Jaego himself.

"There do I wait in the city of the dead,
Here do they trade for years of my soul,
There do I wait, one last thing to be said,
If only you knew what I know.

There do I wait in the City of the Dead,
Where Ankev did fight for his soul,
There do I wait, one last thing to be said,
Wouldn't you like to know?"

The Third Haunting

For Jaego's third haunting, the characters are suddenly wracked with a vision where a mist rises around them, either in their waking hours or in their dreams. The mist clears slightly, and they find they are walking behind Jaego. He walks until he nears a grave covered in freshly turned earth. He points to the gravestone that bears his name. As he points, the ground opens to reveal a broad, damp staircase leading deep into the earth. The sound of rushing waters can be heard somewhere in the cellar-like dankness below.

The characters awaken in the graveyard, standing in full gear amid the many gravestones before an actual opening in the earth. *Detect magic* or other spells and abilities reveal that the opening in the earth is more than it seems and is indeed a portal to another dimension. Each character finds a leaden amulet in the shape of a knot in their hand.

Should the characters brave it at this time, the portal leads to a staircase of 567 steps that takes them to the **Shore of Lost Souls**.

Leaden Knot of the Underworld

Wondrous item, uncommon

While you wear this amulet, you appear as an undead to any creatures or effects that have the ability to detect undead.

Leaden knots are sacred amulets woven into the wrappings of mummies to protect their physical flesh as it is projected into the Underworld before crossing on to the proper afterlife. However, a leaden knot of the Underworld is an amulet fused with a mild protective magic that causes lesser undead such as skeletons, zombies, ghouls, and such lesser spirits to look upon an individual wearing such an amulet as simply another of the dead and to generally ignore them. This is not to say that the dead won't attack someone wearing such an amulet, especially if ordered to do so.

Leaden knots of the Underworld are typically given as gifts from otherworldly powers to clerics of death cults, necromancers, and other travelers of the Underworld to help them avoid unnecessary entanglements with hostile spirits. The amulet affords no other protections.

Part 2: Styx, The Underworld, and the Necropolis of Ankev

The Styx is the vast river of the dead that flows through all the realms of the lower planes, offering access to the various layers of Hell and the Demonic abyss. The various tributaries of the river flow through the Iron Pit of Tartarus, and across the punishing vistas of the Plane of Agony.

The planar edge of the Styx is often referred to as the Underworld, and it is a place where spirits with unfinished business, undead beings, and those who resist their final damnable fates wait. It is said that at the center of this shadowy realm lies the ruined palace of Ankev the arch-lich. Once a servant of Orcus himself, Ankev stood vigil over the Gates of the Dead for centuries on behalf of his corpulent overlord. Eventually, the lich transcended Orcus' control.

It is rumored that Orcus used his wand to destroy Ankev for his insolence, although his death didn't erase Ankev's influence from the world. Parts of his ancient cadaver and gilded panoply still turn up in reliquaries held in esteem by modern necromancers. The City of the Dead at the edge of the Styx still bears his name and stands as a testament to his power and his folly.

Why Adventure in the Necropolis of Ankev?

Many of the beings who inhabit the necropolis carry items of great power, knowledge, or lore. Here, too, is the place where those of evil persuasion may beseech the lords of the Underworld for the raising and resurrecting of their fallen heroes before the Gates of the Dead. Most are turned away or join the minions of death who inhabit the necropolis. Some few are granted their request, but at a price.

Planar Features

As an extension of the plane of the Styx, this vast borderland known by most as the Underworld grants visitors the following bonuses and penalties:

- Undead in the necropolis have full hit points per Hit Die.
- Undead have advantage on all saving throws to resist the effects of Channel Divinity.
- Saving throws versus the effects caused by undead have disadvantage.

Coin of the Realm

In the land of the dead there is little need for mortal coin, with perhaps the exception of vampires who use money to bribe mortals, and mummies who hoard it out of a habit that they had in life. Miserly spirits in life covet treasures in the afterlife though it has no value in the necropolis of Ankev. Instead, the coin of the realm in the Underworld is living life energy. This explains in part its trade for living slaves who are variously sacrificed to Orcus or drained of their life until they join the undead or are consumed utterly by them.

Prices listed for most goods and services are listed in days of life offered by the consumer in exchange for the desired product. For example, a character purchasing a potion or scroll must pay a cost equivalent to its gold piece value in days of his or her mortal life. These days are counted against the maximum age of any character paying the price. If characters spend beyond their years of life and maximum age, they die and are raised as wights or worse.

What the Dead Pay

As the dead have no days of life left to pay to avoid the clutches of the Underworld, they must either find living substitutes to siphon life energy from or they must sacrifice those little pieces that remain of their former life in the form of their living Charisma score. Each point of Charisma sacrificed by the newly dead offers them the opportunity to stay a week longer in the Necropolis before crossing over to the realms of the void to suffer at the hands of Orcus or to be traded to the gods of the other dark realms of the dead. Alternately, they may use their Charisma to haunt someone in the land of the living.

For most of the dead, the choice is simple. They feed off living beings they encounter in the Underworld. Every 10 hit points of damage the dead deal to the living grants them another day of life essence that may be spent in the necropolis before they are forced to move on. The dead who sojourn in the Underworld and reach zero Charisma score become shadows or shades depending on their level before their death.

The Dead vs. the Undead

The dead are fresh souls who find themselves in the Underworld after having been brought across the Styx by a boatman. Most look roughly as they did in life, though signs of their cause of death are evident. Undead are beings who died a horrible death and were brought back as an undead monster by the supernatural forces of the lords of the dead, such as Orcus, or a monster with the ability generate undead.

Dinner of the Dead

Visitors to the Underworld who make a successful DC Intelligence (Religion) check know that any food not brought with the party that is consumed in the land of the dead traps the eater in the realms of the dead forever! It is noted that most visitors must bring their own supply of food or conjure their food through prayer to their deity for manna and fresh water.

There is no save for the curse afflicting those who eat in the land of the dead. The curse may be removed only through the power of a *wish* spell, or by finding other egress through a parallel demi-plane. This plane may be accessed only by entering the realm of Orcus himself! For the dead themselves, the food is a formality; many such as ghouls are filled with insatiable hunger, as vampires are filled with an insatiable thirst for living blood. Neither is satisfied by their meals and continuously crave more, as their tortured and damned souls desire ever to be filled with something that is no longer attainable to them yet is ultimately necessary for their survival!

Vials of Life

These vials are tiny phylacteries that the dead use to store years of life siphoned from the living, or pieces of their eternal soul that they sacrifice for goods and services within the city. The vials each hold one year of life. The vials of life are priceless vessels. Drinking from one of the vessels cures the imbiber for 4d4 + 4 hit points and cures any current non-magical diseases and reduces the physical age of the drinker by 1 year. However, drinking one of the vials while in the Underworld may curse the imbiber to remain as a prisoner of the Underworld forever! Each vial of life beyond the first has its own risks to drinking it. Each vial drunk requires a DC 13 Constitution saving throw. If the saving throw fails, the character ages 10 years for each previous vial that has been drunk. If the number of years exceeds the maximum age for the character's chosen race, he or she dies and rises the following day as a shade lich composed of dust and memory. The DC increases by +1 for every vial beyond the first imbibed by one of the living.

Living Among the Dead

The majority of dead inhabiting the Necropolis of Ankev are still strongly tied to their spirit in so much as they are not generally considered mindless. With the exception of zombies and skeletons created through sacrifice, these beings still have a dim recollection of their life and repeat the same sorts of activities they participated in while alive. They wander, converse, and occasionally collect things. For the most part, the dead yearn for the end of days where they will be called upon by the Lord of the Living Dead to flood forth from the city, along with their brethren in Orcus' home plane, to awaken the unclaimed dead in the land of the living and once and for all scour the universe of the sorrow that the living existence brings. Until that time, they merely wait.

The more powerful of these dead use the relative peace of the Necropolis of Ankev to maneuver for position in the court of Orcus by working out plans to bring about the end of days as it is given to them in verses and prophecy. Vampires, liches, spectres, ghosts, living necromancers, and others scheme with or against one another for their promised fiefdoms in the land of the living once law and good annihilate one another, leaving the world for the dead to rule.

To gain position and strength in the hierarchy of the dead, all require life essence harvested from unfortunate living creatures who find themselves sold or bartered in the Necropolis of Ankev. The highest prizes are sacrificed before the Gate of Orcus that lies beyond the palace-like Mausoleum of Shandar.

1. Shore of Lost Souls and the Tributary

At the bottom of the 576 steps stands a cave on the edge of a narrow underground stream. At the edge of the stream is a mooring post affixed with a length of chain and an iron bell.

This tributary of the River Styx leads to the Necropolis of Ankev. It is accessible only by those who would have business with the dead. For example, a party of heroes seeking to catch the cohorts of a fallen enemy before they attempt to raise their foe at the Gates of the Dead may claim business in the Necropolis.

When the iron bell is rung, a skiff large enough to ferry the passengers arrives in 1d4 rounds. The boatman is a **charonadaemon** (see **Appendix**) who asks what business the characters have on the Shore of Lost Souls. Individuals seeking knowledge or who are searching for a treasure map, item, or piece of information inside the necropolis may declare this as their reason for seeking Ankev's hidden city. The charonadaemon demands 2 pieces of silver or a magic item of at least +1 value from the riders. Once paid, he allows the characters to board his skiff and sets out for the Bone Gate.

Characters foolish enough to kill the charonadaemon find themselves lost on the River Styx. Who knows what shores of the dead their skiff eventually lands upon?

2. Bone Gate

The **Bone Gate** (see **Appendix**) stands atop a hill a short distance from the quay where the boatman disembarks passengers. Jagged walls made up of bone and skulls from hundreds of different sentient beings speak in unison, challenging visitors about their purpose in the land of the dead.

Travelers are asked what business they have in the land of the dead. The Bone Gate offers characters a second chance to turn back. If no answer is given, the gate does not open. If a poor answer is given, the visitors are asked to leave. If the visitors attack the gate, they likely destroy it, but find that the planar nexus is then closed to them for 24 hours, denying them entrance to the land of the dead until the gate reforms. If the gate is destroyed, nothing lies beyond it save a simple cave. Entering the cave deposits the visitors back upon the quay. A character making a successful DC 16 Intelligence (Religion) check recognizes the temporary closure of the nexus.

If the gate is destroyed, it becomes a one-way gate that leads out of the demi-plane and directly back to the land of the living rather than a two-way gate leading in and out. Roll once on the Ghoul Canyon Random Encounters table while visitors wait for the gate to reform.

3. The Ghoul Canyon

This half-mile-long canyon extends beyond the Bone Gate. It is dotted with crumbling charnel houses and age-worn tombstones shrouded in sickly-looking green vapors that rise from jagged fissures in the ground. Dark figures scurry around the edges of the canyon.

Ghoul Canyon Random Encounters

1d12	Encounter
1	2d8 ghouls
2	1d4 ghasts
3	1d4+4 giant rats
4	1d4+2 ghoulish giant rats (see Appendix)
5	1d4 rat swarms
6	Brain rat (see Appendix)
7–12	No Encounter

4. Amien's Keep

Amien's Keep stands in the corner of a large stone grotto. More a large three-story mansion than an actual fortified structure, it is surrounded by a wall of polished green marble. The keep of the **ghoul lord** (with *+2 mace* and AC 18 from *+1 half plate*, see **Appendix**) Amien is located along the eastern expanse of the cavern where he exerts his own form of maddening authority over the denizens of the canyon. Although under the direct authority of Shandar, Amien rules as he sees fit, capturing those unfortunate living entities who do not pay his toll and trading them in the necropolis for things to fulfill his own perverse needs.

The keep itself is decrepit and in decay. Each floor has roughly 2d4 usable rooms, and there is a 50% chance per room that the characters encounter 1d6 **ghouls**, 1d4 **ghasts**, or a structural issue requiring a DC 14 Dexterity saving throw versus a trap to avoid 14 (4d6) bludgeoning damage from broken timbers and rubble.

Treasure: Amien's treasury includes three 1,000 gp emeralds, a 1,000 gp opal, 2,500 gp in an iron chest, an oil painting of Amien in life standing amid ghouls worth 12,000 gp, a *potion of giant strength* (fire giant), and 6 vials of life, each containing a month of life siphoned off unfortunate travelers caught in the Ghoul Canyon.

Amien charges a year of life to mortal passers-by who cross through his realm into the necropolis itself.

5. Outer Slums

The outermost ring of the necropolis consists of the smashed mausoleums and broken tombs of the lesser dead and those wandering souls who are newly arrived in the city. These new dead often seek sanctuary among those spirits yet to be called to the inner rings of the city — and for good reason. Each spirit knows that the closer one gets to the Mouth of Orcus, the closer one is to losing whatever shred of living memory still resides in one's decaying brain.

The Outer Slums are separated from the Lower Ward by a 10-foot-high wall topped with jagged iron spikes.

6. The Bone Mill

Bones picked clean of all flesh are piled from floor to ceiling among the walls of this cursed charnel house. Contingents of mindless zombies on treadmills turn the great millwheel that grinds the bones of dismembered skeletons to dust.

Considered a good shopping place for necromancers seeking a quick complement of skeletons to "bone out" their army, the Bone Yard is also an excellent source of ground bone for use in bone meal or material spell components used in the necromantic arts.

A warehouse in the back contains a plethora of additional bones, though none make up a complete skeleton. They are instead the collected remains of a great number of sentient beasts.

Lysipus the **bone cobbler** (see **Appendix**) runs the Bone Mill. He keeps an amulet designed to store the life essence of his clients. His bone sells for one year of life per wagonload, though he pays half that for fresh bones brought to him in bulk.

7. Leathers of the Flesh

This slaughterhouse trades evenly with the Bone Yard for any "incomplete" corpses sold to them. Leathers of the Flesh is a squat stone building with a chimney that constantly spouts the foul-smelling odors of the tanners' trade. Within may be heard the moans and whimpers of those resigned to the terror of the last hours of their existence. Leathers of the Flesh is operated by Cainor the **skin stitcher** (see **Appendix**), a wicked being whose greatest pleasure is peeling his victims and devouring their flesh. Cainor makes exquisite leather armor that is highly sought by those who care not that the skin defending them was once the skin of a living, thinking being. Cainor sells his extra scraps for parchment at the neighboring bookbinder.

Armor of Undeath

Armor (leather), legendary (requires attunement)

This armor is crafted from the flesh of humanoid beings and is as soft and supple as one's own skin. While wearing it, you gain a +3 bonus to your armor class. In addition, you have advantage on any saving throws to resist the effects of necromantic spells and touch attacks made by undead creatures. The armor is decidedly evil in its very nature, however, and you have disadvantage on any Charisma checks other than Intimidation checks made to influence a creature who recognize the leather's source for what it is.

Wraith Armor

Armor (leather), legendary (requires attunement)

While wearing this armor, you gain a +2 bonus to your armor class. Once per day, you can assume the incorporeal form of a wraith for up to one minute. While in wraith form, you can use a bonus action to make an unarmed attack that deals 1d8 necrotic damage.

8. Lower Ward

The Lower Ward is separated by a simple, unattended iron gate that marks the boundary of the Outer Slums from the city proper. The Lower Ward rises along the hill upon which the necropolis sits. Made up mostly of row after row of gravestones, single-occupant mausoleums, and aboveground sarcophagi, the Lower Ward's population is mostly **skeletons**, **zombies**, and other lesser undead. While these beings are considered mindless in the land of the living, in Ankev's realm they possess a slightly more rudimentary intelligence, though their conversations and aims are akin to those of living commoners. They typically go about their business, paying no mind to living visitors unless bothered or if they believe they are strong enough to dine on the flesh of the living. Well-armed visitors, those displaying holy symbols, or those doused in holy water are left alone unless ordered to act by a more powerful being. Thousands of skeletons, zombies, and other lost souls wander the Lower Ward or simply rest within a mausoleum or disturbed grave.

9. Inn of the Moldering Corpse

A decrepit brick pile hung with the sign of a rotting corpse sits on a desolate street in the suburbs, butting up against the walls of Ankev proper.

This inn and tavern serves as a waystation for those seeking entry to the necropolis. Within its walls are a variety of visitors from other times and planes of existence, all with some business within the gated city. A variety of services are offered, including rooms and "food" of sorts, though it is the food of the dead and offers its own unique risks for the unwary traveler.

The Inn of the Moldering Corpse is operated by Grall Tabrel, a **ghost** who has seemingly always run the inn. Grall has a gravelly voice and is polite to visitors who do not attempt to cause problems with him or his establishment. Grall is a fairly good source of information about living visitors and the newly dead since he doesn't care about their plots, concerns, or worries. His freedom with information often proves to be a two-edged sword for those seeking more discreet lodgings, though he may be bribed for the equivalent of one day of life per day of stay in his inn to "keep quiet." Since no other lodgings are in the suburbs, and camping in the Ghoul Canyon brings near-constant attacks, most visitors resign themselves to paying Grall's prices.

Services

Room for the Night	1 day of life essence
Pickled Halfling Brains	2 days life essence
Raw Humanoid	1 day life essence
Bonemeal Bread	1 day life essence per loaf, grants a +1 bonus versus the effects of necromantic spells for 24 hours.
Living Blood Slave (not to be drained to death!)	2 years of life essence or 200 gp in magic items. (Typically reserved for vampires or others who feast on blood.)

Renting a room at the Inn of the Moldering Corpse guarantees that the renter is left unmolested by any of the other denizens of the demi-plane, unless the characters happen to be wanted for high crimes in the necropolis itself. It does not, however, offer protection against other visitors, so let the renter beware!

Current Visitors

The following characters are currently holed up at the Inn of the Moldering Corpse:

Sir Ulatuan and the Wights: Sir Ulatuan is a **fallen paladin** (see **Appendix**) of Orcus who keeps the company of a gathering of 6 **wights**. Lord Ulatuan goes forth and spreads the gospel of the Lord of the Dead in hopes of achieving the grace of becoming a death knight upon his dying breath. Ulatuan is currently working as a bounty hunter of sorts, collecting lost souls from the shores of the Styx or the Valley of Ghouls and delivering them to the Temple of Orcus.

Lord Ulatuan may be hired to track down Jaego's whereabouts. He charges five years of life for the task, and characters must provide their own vials of life to seal the bargain. Ulatuan finds Jaego's location in 1d4 days but has a 50% chance of cutting a deal with Shandar to deliver the characters to the lich queen.

Hukeesh the Necromancer: Hukeesh (see **Appendix**) seeks entry to Mïzć Kü Tanük but has yet to collect the amount of life required to barter entrance without succumbing to the touch of death himself. Hukeesh may offer his services as a guide in the Necropolis of Ankev for a year's worth of life essence. He claims deep knowledge of the newly dead and could lead characters to the soul they seek. Hukeesh would trade the information for either admission to Mïzć Kü Tanük or free access to five necromancy spells of 2nd–4th level.

10. Shadow Gate

This planar gate offers passage from the Underworld to the Plane of Shadow, a plane marked by its ghostly resemblance to the world of the living. The gates are guarded by a contingent of 2d8 **shadows** who deny entrance to the realm of the Shadow Lords. The living must bring one of the dead to act as a spirit guide with them to pass into the realm of shadow. Or they must be willing to sacrifice a portion of their life essence (in the form of Strength) to enter the darkness. Those submitting to the touch of the shadows are drained of 1d4 points of Strength before they are allowed to pass into the plane beyond.

11. The Sign of the Grinning Skull

This boardinghouse caters to the warrior caste, where skeletal warriors rub elbows with bloody bones as they drink their mugs of dust and revel in tales of how they came to be. The grinning skull is the place to go for an aspiring necromancer looking to recruit unholy warriors of the undead to serve as officers in their armies.

The Sign of the Grinning Skull is run by Malago, a **skeletal warrior** (see **Appendix**) who dutifully connects patrons with undead mercenary leaders and their cohorts. Each mercenary commands a squad of 4d8 **skeletons** or **zombies**, or 2d8 **ghouls**.

Rooms can be rented in this dusty mausoleum as well for two days of life essence per day of lodging. The renter is protected from assault by other patrons so long as he or she obeys the house rules and causes no trouble with the other guests.

Hiring the Undead

The following are some examples of undead found in the Sign of the Grinning Skull and the cost in life essence to hire them.

Undead (see **Appendix**)	Cost to Hire
1d4 **Black Skeletons**	1 year of life each for one year of service
2d4 **Juju Zombies**	1 year of life each for one year of service.
Barrow Wight	1 year of life for 3 months of service

12. Kreal's Bookbinder

Kreal (**mage**) is a renowned bookbinder who sells blank scrolls and magic books crafted of dwarf, elf, human, dragon, and other various rare skins. Such skins are much sought after by demonologists, necromancers, and other magic-users of the darker arts. A trio of deft **goblins** assists him in crafting his handmade books. The goblins were long ago fed the food of the dead and can no longer leave the Necropolis of Ankev.

Kreal sells materials used in the crafting of magical books and scrolls.

Items for Sale

Item	Cost in Life Essence
Ink	100 days of life per bottle
Human skin	25 days of life per page
Elf skin	75 days of life per page (a spell cast from a scroll written on this paper is cast at a spell slot one higher than the minimum)
Dragon skin	200 days of life per page (a spell cast from a scroll written on this paper is cast at a spell slot two higher than the minimum)
Demon, devil, or angel skin	500 days of life per page (a spell cast from a scroll written on this paper is cast at a spell slot three higher than the minimum)

13. Middle Ward

Larger numbers of the living dwell in the Middle Ward than the Upper and Lower Wards, as it is the location of the Temple of Orcus, The Nightmare Consortium, and the fabled Mïzć Kü Tanük University and its fabled library. Aside from the campus and the apartments of Orcus' acolytes, and the crypts of the university faculty, a few other shops or amenities are found here for those beings not interested in the affairs of Orcus' living worshippers.

14. The Nightmare Consortium: Hauntings for Hire

The Nightmare Consortium is a loose coalition of spirits who hire themselves out to perform haunting activities in the land of the living. Typically, necromancers or evil warlords seek them to serve as guardians of their keeps. Wicked nobles also use them to haunt the homes of their political rivals.

Their typical term of service is one year for each living soul traded, or one week for each day of life traded. As usual, the most common form of payment is in prisoners traded to the consortium, who in turn trade the unfortunate prisoners at the Temple of Orcus, thus furthering their own goal in achieving their paradise in the realm of Orcus.

The nightmare consortium houses a variety of phantoms, spectres, wraiths, poltergeists, and ghosts, all with a particular penchant for the horrific. Business with the consortium is managed by Ramn Pujab (**mage**) an illusionist with some training in the necromantic arts. Ramn interviews potential customers, fixing them up with the particular spirit of their needs. Once the needs of the customer are established, they are given a soul jar housing the undead intended to fulfill their purpose.

The Nightmare Consortium Spirits

At any given time, 1d4 of the following spirits are on the premises of the Nightmare Consortium. Hiring them costs life essence.

Undead	Cost in Life Essence
Ghosts	1 year of life per month of service
Wraiths	1 year of life per 3 months of service
Specters	1 year of life per 6 months of service

15. Necromancer's Touch

The necromancer's touch is managed by Zara Darksilk, a **drider** who weaves most of the clothes herself. The shop features fashions and accessories for the discerning necromancer. Robes, capes, turbans, caps, black lipstick, and lace gloves can all be found here to help the living add that fresh "touch of death" to their ensemble.

Sample Items

Item	Cost in Life Essence
Velvet cowl	50 days of life
Lace gloves	50 days of life
Red and black velvet mantlet embroidered with rubies	2,000 days of life (affords a +1 bonus to armor class)
Black velvet robes	100 days of life
Drider silk pantaloons	250 days of life
Diamond crusted eyepatch	500 days of life
Thigh-high leather boots (red or black)	200 days of life

16. The Temple of Orcus

This open-air temple is carved in the shape of a pair of clawed skeletal hands and a grinning skull. A bowl held between the hands turns any corpse thrown into it into a zombie, skeleton, or other undead based on the victim's hit dice. Adroculus the Sacrificer (**emeritus chaplain** with a *rod of animate dead* and +2 on all saving throws against enchantments, charms, and mind control effects, see **Appendix**) oversees the temple's day-to-day activities. He is assisted by a pair of **acolytes** and guarded by a squad of 20 **guards** from the Undying Legion that he commands utterly. Adroculus keeps an apartment in a mansion-sized mausoleum not far from the temple and awaits the day when his god calls him to join the undead as one of their own.

Typically, a line of 2d12 chained slaves (**commoners**, unless something more interesting suits your fancy) awaits sacrifice upon the steps leading to the bowl. Among these are an additional 2d20 lost dead who have run out of Charisma, vials of life, or hope — or all three — and find their spirit forms further mutilated during the sacrifice.

The altar at the top of the steps is where Adroculus cuts out the hearts of the wretched victims, casting them to the milling crowd of **zombies**, **ghouls**, and **vampire spawn** who often wrestle for their morsels. Upon completing the sacrifice, Adroculus reawakens the dead as zombies, skeletons, or some greater undead with an enchanted rod given him by Shandar. The horrid sacrifices end when the daily charges of the rod are expelled.

The bowl of the temple is an open one-way portal leading to layers of the Abyss ruled by Orcus. Spirits unclaimed by other gods that are cast through the portal soon find themselves turned into dretches, quasits, or larvae of the lower planes.

Rod of Animate Dead

Rod, legendary (requires attunement)

This rod has 7 charges. As an action, you can use one or more charges to animate the following undead. Appropriate corpses or souls must be present.

1 charge: you animate a corpse as Wa skeleton or zombie.
3 charges: you animate 2d20 ghouls
3 charges: you animate 2d10 vampire spawn
4 charges: you animate a pile of corpses as a zombie horde
  (see **Appendix**)

Typically, those who come to the Necropolis of Ankev to raise their dead allies are turned away by Orcus. In this event, they are directed to find Adroculus, who offers transformation to undeath instead. His price to perform the ritual is 999 days of life or a living sacrifice of a sentient being to Orcus.

17. Hennian the Glassblower

Hennian (**night hag**) crafts vials of life from sand collected from the shores of the River Styx. Empty vials of life cost a year of life to purchase but may be used to absorb life from those willing to give up their years to fill these curious bottles.

Treasure: Hennian has four vials of life with a year of life in each, a *cloak of elvenkind*, a *ring of jumping*, 1,800 gp, and a ruby ring worth 350 gp.

18. Mïzć Kü Tanük Institute

Mïzć Kü Tanük Institute is a secretive and highly sought institute for study of necromancy and the occult. Necromancers from various planes often seek the Necropolis of Ankev merely to attend courses of study or to purchase spells from the fabled library.

Lectures are given on occasion by liches and other masters of the undead, including such foul luminaries as Jhedophar, Athransma, and Earl Damien Aerim.

Admittance to the institute requires a year of life. Any spells or knowledge to manufacture magic items requires additional payment, either in months, sacrifices, or trade in magical items.

New necromancer spells may be scribed into spellbooks for the cost of one month of life per level of the spell. Thus, a 1st-level spell requires sacrificing one month of life, while a 9th-level spell requires nine months of life.

The institute is the only place in the Necropolis of Ankev where leaden knots can be purchased. The amulets cost one year of life each.

The institute is administered by the **ghost** of Professor Axeworm Armitage III. Axeworm served as a living sage when the institute was founded and has remained at his post for nearly 400 years.

He is assisted by 12 **wraiths** who ensure that the books are not harmed and that visiting students respect the sanctity of the institution.

Axeworm is privy to a great deal of information about the comings and goings of spirits and the political winds of the necropolis. For five years of life, he shares the location of Jaego should the characters ask.

The corpses of the wraiths are buried in the faculty crypts on the campus grounds. Their tombs contain a variety of treasures that they held dear in life. However, searching the crypts without first dealing with the wraiths could prove problematic as the wraiths appear in 1d4 rounds to defend their worldly treasures.

Treasure: four vials of life worth one year of life each, a ruby monocle that casts *scorching ray* 1/day, *gloves of protection from poison* (+4 to saving throws vs. poison), a *staff of thunder and lightning*, a *robe of shielding* (cast *shield* 3/day), 24 sp, and a *gem of seeing*.

19. Upper Ward

The tombs, crypts, and mausoleums of the upper ward are much larger and of higher quality though smaller in number than those found in the Middle and Lower wards. Elite visitors are guided to the Ruby Chalice for shows and events or sent to the Bloodless Court to seek lodging more discerning and sublime than those found in the Lower Ward or the suburban outskirts of the necropolis.

20. Adroculus' Manor

This manor house serves as the home of Adroculus the High Priest of Orcus. The multiroom structure is tended by 4 lesser priests of Orcus (as **cult fanatics**) and is guarded by a force of 10 unholy paladins (as **holy knights**, see **Appendix**) in service of the lord of the dead.

The doors to Adroculus' private chambers are cursed. An uninvited creature that passes through the doors becomes cursed. While cursed, the creature automatically fails any saving throw against the effect of an undead creature. The curse can be removed with *remove curse*. The curse can be detected prior to passing through the doors with a successful DC 18 Intelligence (Arcana) check while investigating the doors.

Within his chambers is a locked bronze-bound chest trapped with contact poison smeared on the lock. The poison can be noted with a successful DC 20 Intelligence (Investigation) check. If the poison is touched, the creature touching it must succeed on a DC 16 Constitution saving throw or collapse in a near-death state for 2d6 hours. The poison can be safely removed with a successful DC 15 Dexterity check with thieves' tools. The lock can be opened with a successful DC 18 Dexterity check with thieves' tools. The chest contains 10 vials each containing a year of life.

21. The Ruby Chalice

The Ruby Chalice is a vampire-run cabaret catering to upscale clientele and intelligent undead who still have a bit of zeal and zest for life, particularly for the life essence and blood of the living!

Romeo Nacht (**vampire** with a *+2 rapier*), an agent of the Underguild, is the proprietor of the Ruby Chalice. He is assisted by 6 **vampire spawn**. Romeo has allies among many slaving organizations on a dozen different planes who fill his quota of fresh hot blood and timid, sorrowful souls to appease the tastes of his clientele. One such organization with which Romeo is connected is the Underguild and their infamous chain of taverns and bordellos.

The cabaret features entertainment twice daily in the form of skits, dance ensembles, and dirges performed by bands of the living and the dead. One of the more popular shows is a comedy performance put on by Zuriel Von Dokker, the **wraith** of a wizard left unburied by his fellow adventurers after they plundered his corpse for the gear and loot he carried.

Equally popular are the Juliettes, Romeo's dancing girls, who do a cancan dance. These comely **vampire spawn** each fell in love with Romeo in life, were willingly turned, and are now loyal to him above all else. The dancers are known to charm living visitors to the Ruby Chalice into sacrificing their blood and life essence.

Unlike most other locales within the Necropolis of Ankev, Romeo is still very much addicted to the trappings of life, especially magic items, and often takes payment in magic or living slaves in lieu of the years of life that other denizens accept.

Wares: Aside from lively entertainment, the following succulent items may be selected off the Ruby Chalice's menu.

Menu Items

Eating the food at the Ruby Chalice comes with specific risks and rewards. The deleterious effects of the food served may be cured with a *remove curse* or *lesser restoration* spell.

Living Blood Slave (not to be drained to death!)	2 years of life essence or 200 gp in magic items per draught. (Typically reserved for vampires or others who feast on blood.)
Nether Ambrosia	There is nothing so sweet as the food of the gods. Sweeter still is the food of the dead. Mortals consuming the nether ambrosia must make a successful DC 15 Constitution saving throw or be struck dead by the rush of flavors. Those who die rise as wights within 24 hours.
Midnight Wine	The wine of the underworld, midnight wine forces deep and troubled dreams upon the living. The dreams are sometimes portentous, but as often as not lead to a long coma and slow death. Imbibers must make a successful DC 16 Constitution saving throw or fall into a coma lasting 1d4 days. At the end of each day, the drinker must make another saving throw. If this fails, the drinker dies and rises as a wraith upon the start of the next evening. Drinkers who succeed on their saving throw are faced with visions that award them knowledge of their next dangerous encounter, the solution to an upcoming puzzle or trap, or a free reroll of their choice.
Grave Truffles	Also called coffin fruit, this fungus grows upon old, decaying coffins. The grave truffle is a true delicacy to the dead. Those who can withstand the initial bite of the grave truffle gain an increased fortitude against the effects of the dead. Eaters must make a successful DC 15 Constitution saving throw after ingesting grave truffles. Failure results in 17 (4d6) necrotic damage. On a successful save, the eater gains a +2 to saving throws versus the effects of undead for 24 hours.
Death by Chocolate	This desert is favored by fiends of Hell and the Abyss for its pure decadence. When eaten by mortals, this chocolate cake, pudding, and liquor syrup delicacy fills them with euphoria and a sense of satisfaction and vigor unlike anything else they have ever experienced. Eating a treat meant for the damned, however, comes at a cost. As the flavor of death by chocolate is so intense, no other food may ever sate their hunger again. Mortals must make a successful DC 17 Constitution saving throw or waste away, losing 1d4 points of Constitution per day as they uncontrollably shed weight until they eventually die from starvation. On a successful save, the character gains a +2 bonus to their Constitution and Charisma scores that lasts for 24 hours.

22. Garrison of the Undying Legion

This barracks houses 30 **fear guards** (see **Appendix**) led by Lord Kartillion the Heathen, a **demonic knight** (see **Appendix**) who rides a stout **nightmare**.

Once a paladin of law and justice, Lord Kartillion was driven mad during a long-forgotten crusade during which he was given orders to sack cities that had surrendered and to put prisoners to the sword. After murdering his fellow generals and his crown prince in a fit of rage, Kartillion swore allegiance to the banner Orcus, Lord of the Dead, before leading his men on a rampaging crusade of bloodlust and murder across three kingdoms of Libynos. Kartillion and his core of 30 battle-mad knights met their end at the end of the lances of the Numedan cavalry nearly 500 years ago.

In death, Kartillion has crawled his way from the pits of the Abyss and now commands the damned souls of his old brigade once more in the form of Shandar's own private police force.

23. Ruins of Ankev's Palace

A field of rubble is all that remains of the once-mighty palace of Ankev, former chosen herald of Orcus. The field retains naught but broken stone since the destruction of Ankev's palace and the rending of his form across the cosmos.

24. Quad of the Taharqo

These 400-foot-tall pyramids form a quad to the south of the Mausoleum of Shandar and serve as the resting place of Peimeroe Taharqo (**mummy lord**) and his 3 **mummy** sons. These famed warrior princes of ancient Khemit now hold spectral court here for all eternity.

Taharqo and his sons seldom venture from their tombs, but when they do, it is in force, with the four of them fighting in unison as they did when they established the southern dynastic line. The four are able to open a gate to the Astral Plane where Ammit and Anubis wait to judge the heart and soul of those who become lost on their way to the afterlife.

Taharqo opens the gate to the Scales of Judgement for 10 years of life or 10 points of Charisma.

Treasure: *Potion of giant strength* (frost giant), *marvelous pigments*, *spell scroll* of *plane shift*, *spell scroll* of *contingency*, 18,000 gp, *robe of the archmagi*, and 20 vials of life.

25. Mausoleum of Shandar

As Ankev fell, so did Shandar rise from his ashes. A faithful sorceress steeped in the necromantic arts, Shandar performed the rites and rituals of eternal undeath as soon as the first touches of age began to stretch their skein across her brow. Shandar had studied at the foot of many of the moldering lich lords, absorbing their magic and studying the craft of their phylacteries. She drank deeply of the living souls bartered in the necropolis at the edge of the Abyss to extend her own age unnaturally.

For a living corpse, Shandar almost appears to be a freshly fed vampire, save for a waxy sheen and the thick stench of formaldehyde she exudes like a sickly perfume. Shandar lazily observes the happenings within the necropolis from within the depths of her labyrinthine tomb.

The mausoleum's maze is said to be controlled by the Shandar's own thoughts, requiring a genius to navigate the twisting passageways without becoming completely lost. Aside from the ever-changing maze, the mausoleum is also filled with traps that are mechanical and magical in nature.

Characters must make five successful DC 20 Intelligence checks to find their way through the maze. On a failed check, the characters become lost and encounter a trap. Suggested traps are listed below. After five successful checks, the characters find themselves in Shandar's crypt.

Maze Traps

1.   **Smashing Wall Trap:** This trap is triggered by the third figure to step onto a hidden plate, which can be noticed with a successful DC 18 Wisdom (Perception) check. Triggering the trap deals 55 (10d10) bludgeoning damage to everyone within a 10-foot area of the smashing walls. The trap may be disarmed by wedging the plate so that it cannot depress. Successfully disarming the plate requires a successful DC 14 Dexterity check with thieves' tools.

2.   **Lighting Field Trap:** This trap is set off by a change in electromagnetic energy brought about by living beings passing through the field. The floor and walls of this area are lined with copper inlay that spell out the words "Goodbye, Thieves," in elvish, dwarvish, gnomish, common, and diabolical tongues. Noticing the writing requires a successful DC 15 Wisdom (Perception) check. The magical nature of the trap can be detected with a *detect magic* spell or a successful DC 18 Intelligence (Arcana) check. Characters can disable the trap with a *dispel magic* spell or by rubbing wool on the word "good" in the diabolical script to neutralize the field's polarity.

3.   **Pit Trap:** This can be noted with a successful DC 15 Wisdom (Perception) check to notice. It may be disabled with a successful DC 15 Dexterity check with thieves' tools, preventing it from tipping and dropping the characters 50 feet into a 5-foot-by-5-foot cube of **green slime**. Characters who fall into the slime take 11 (2d10) acid damage per round as the enzymes devour their flesh and gear. The sides of the wall are covered in a slick greasy substance that make it a challenge to climb out of the pit, requiring a DC 18 Strength (Athletics) check.

4.   **Hall of Spears Trap:** Phalanxes of spears are hidden in the walls of this 30-foot-long hallway. These spears come from the floor, ceiling, or walls. The spear holes can be noted with a successful DC 17 Wisdom (Perception) check. They are cleverly hidden in carvings featuring the grandeur of Shandar's rise to power. The phalanxes can be disabled with a hidden lever buried inside a carved skull at the outset of each end of the hallway. The lever can be found with a successful DC 15 Intelligence (Investigation) check. Failure to notice or disarm the trap allows the spears to "attack" characters in a 10-foot area. The spears attack each character in a 10-foot area at a +12 to hit. On a hit, the target takes 21 (6d6) piercing damage and is impaled. While impaled it is restrained. Removing the spear from the target causes an additional 14 (4d6) piercing damage unless the person removing it makes a successful DC 15 Wisdom (Medicine) check.

5.   **Wall of Ice Trap:** Sharp-eyed characters notice a rune of cold on the floor and ceiling of the hallway with a successful DC 15 Wisdom (Perception) check, or automatically note a magical aura over the area should a *detect magic* spell be in effect. The trap may be disabled with *dispel magic* cast wth a successful DC 15 spell attack roll. Bearing a torch through this section of the corridor causes walls of ice to spring up 10 feet in front and behind them. The ice quickly flows across the floor and ceiling around them, thus narrowing the tunnel and effectively trapping them within a 10-foot-by-20-foot ice cube. As the ice spreads across the floor, characters must make a successful DC 20 Dexterity saving throw or suffer 35 (10d6) cold damage. Characters within the block of ice continue to take 18 (5d6) cold damage per round.

6.   **Monster Summoning:** Characters notice a rune of cold and a rune of summoning on the floor and ceiling of the hallway they are about to enter with a successful DC 15 Wisdom (Perception) check, or they automatically note a magical aura over the area should a *detect magic* spell be in effect. The trap may be disabled with *dispel magic*. Crossing into the area without noticing the rune triggers the trap, which summons a **black bulette** (see **Appendix**) that attacks immediately.

Shandar's Crypt

Shandar the **lich** resides within her large stone crypt, spending her hours observing the goings-on of the city with her *crystal ball of mind reading* and preparing herself for the inevitable decay of her flesh. The crypt walls are hung with black velvet. Under the velvet are a dozen silver mirrors where the once beautiful but now waxen queen of the Necropolis of Ankev once observed her comely form.

Shandar leaves the confines of her crypt only when meting out punishment within the necropolis. Such events tend to be few and far between, though it is not unusual for her to send her **imp** Rawhide out to the city to collect a misplaced soul for her amusement.

Treasure: Shandar's treasury is hidden within a *portable hole* found folded into a book upon the bookshelf standing next to her crypt. Within the *portable hole* are 3,300 gp, 1,000 platinum, three sapphires worth 1,000 gp each, one diamond worth 2,000 gp, a fire opal worth 1,000 gp, a map of the City of Brass with the address of Rah'po Dehj marked on it, a *potion of supreme healing*, a *spell scroll* of *plane shift*, a *potion of speed*, and 10 vials of life each containing 1 year of life each.

Where is Jaego?

It is left up to you where to place Jaego, but listed below are locations and reasons why he might be trapped there. Characters will need to use their role-playing skills to locate Jaego, and access to his spirit may be contingent on completing a quest for the being currently holding his spirit hostage.

Interviewing Denizens of the Necropolis

Characters may talk to the random dead they encounter in the Necropolis of Ankev to determine the whereabouts of Jaego's spirit. Talking to a random intelligent undead off the street has a 1-in-20 chance per day of giving them a clue to his whereabouts.

Talking to proprietors of one of the city's shops or taverns offers a 5-in-20 chance of receiving useful information about Jaego's current location.

Hiring Lord Ulatuan or Hukeesh guarantees Jaego's location is revealed, but comes with its own dangers. Alternately, the characters may visit the institute to ask Axeworm if he knows anything.

Prisoner of Amien

Amien noticed that the newly dead Jaego was taking great efforts to contact the living, especially for one who had been in the Underworld for such a short period of time. Amien captured Jaego's Underworld form and now holds it in his manor house. Amien demands that the characters bring him a willing sacrifice to Orcus. Either that, or he requires 20 filled vials of life in exchange for their friend's restless spirit.

Held by Adroculus

Adroculus is aware that Jaego reached beyond the land of the dead for some form of aid. If approached, Adroculus offers to trade Jaego's spirit for one of the living characters, whom he then intends to sacrifice to Orcus.

Prisoner in the Ruby Chalice

Romeo Nacht is holding the spirit of Jaego. He is willing to trade Jaego's spirit if someone agrees to serve him for a year as his willing blood slave. He'll also accept a powerful magic item of your choice.

In the Shadow Lands

Jaego's spirit hid on the Plane of Shadow but was captured by the Shadow Demon Shoren and is currently being held in the city of Dehenet (detailed in *The Sword of Air* by **Frog God Games**).

Shandar's Mausoleum

Jaego is currently a prisoner in Shandar's Mausoleum. Shandar demands that the characters go forth and recover one of the Letek're stones from the Isle of Eliphaz (detailed in **Isle of Eliphaz** in *Quests of Doom Volume 2* from **Frog God Games**).

Remember that the above are simply suggestions. You may have a better location or may use a plot hook more appropriate to your campaign world.

Jaego is Found!

Jaego's spirit is weak and much diminished due to his great expenditure of Charisma to make contact with the characters from the Underworld. Once Jaego is recovered, he tells them the story of a secret diary he hid behind some bricks in the booth of his favorite tavern. Jaego thanks them for being such good friends to him in life, and for serving as an inspiration to his art. He explains that the diary contains damning information about the true parentage of an heir to a pair of noble houses and leaves it to the characters to decide what is best to do with the diary and the information contained therein. He feels responsible for the contents of the diary but believes the characters will know best what to do and has resigned himself to joining the damned either in the Abyss or the Hells.

After revealing his truth and the secret location of the diary, Jaego thanks them again for what they have done for him both in life and in death. With that, his spirit seemingly fades away.

The Return

Characters may return to the surface world by summoning a boatman and paying him his fee of two silvers each.

Choices

The ledger reveals that Jaego is the true father of Lord Mercier and Earl Brodchek's grandson. The Council of Reme ordered Mercier's daughter to marry Earl Brodchek's son as a means of creating peace between the warring families. The Brodchek family suspected something was amiss when the child was born eight months after the wedding. The child was small at birth, and the wetnurses explained that the child was simply born too early. Brodchek was still not convinced and received word that the Mercier's longtime herald had left the count's banner. He dispatched his agents to track down Jaego for questioning. The search took years because Jaego had done a good job of covering his tracks — until recently.

In the meantime, the marriage between the Mercier and Brodchek family resulted in a truce of sorts as the business and political rivals attempted to move past their old differences. Jaego's diary would no doubt spark a broad conflict that would disrupt trade and destabilize the northwestern region of Akados for years to come.

The characters could reveal the truth. Or they could destroy the diary and keep Jaego's secret and the peace. The choice is up to them. However, if the characters destroy the diary, award them 1,000 additional experience points. Jaego's spirit visits them one last time and thanks them for their choice. He then moves on to a happier afterlife than was offered by Orcus or the forces of the Lightbringer.

Further Adventure

The characters may continue their exploration of the Underworld for as long as they wish, though their time may be limited due to a lack of proper provisions and the prescripts about eating in the land of the dead. If they return to the Styx, they may summon the boatman to take them back to the land of the living. When they step off the boat onto the shores of the Styx, they instead find themselves at the site of Jaego's grave. Their friendship with Jaego may eventually reach the ears of Mercier and Brodchek, meaning the characters may find themselves facing assassins and bounty hunters working on behalf of both nobles.

APPENDIX

Creatures that appear in this adventure that are not in the Fifth Edition SRD are detailed below.

BARROW WIGHT

Medium undead, chaotic evil

Armor Class 14 (studded leather)
Hit Points 45 (6d8 + 18)
Speed 30 ft.

STR	DEX	CON	INT	WIS	CHA
16 (+3)	14 (+2)	16 (+3)	10 (+0)	13 (+1)	15 (+2)

Skills Perception +3, Stealth +4
Damage Resistances necrotic; bludgeoning, piercing and slashing from nonmagical weapons that are not silvered
Damage Immunities poison
Condition Immunities exhaustion, poisoned
Senses darkvision 60 ft., passive Perception 13
Languages the language it knew in life
Challenge 3 (700 XP)

Insanity Gaze. If a creature starts its turn within 30 feet of the barrow wight and the two of them can see each other, the barrow wight can force the creature to make a DC 13 Wisdom saving throw if the barrow wight is not incapacitated. On a failed save, the creature is affected by a short term madness effect for 1 minute. Determine the effect from the table below.

d100	Effect (lasts 1 minute)
01-20	The target retreats into its mind and becomes paralyzed. The effect ends if the creature takes any damage.
21-30	The creature is incapacitated, and can only scream, laugh, or weep hysterically.
31-40	The creature is frightened and must use its actions to flee from the source of its fear.
41-50	The creature babbles incoherently and cannot speak normally or cast spells.
51-60	The creature must use its action to attack the nearest creature.
61-70	The creature hallucinates vividly, incurring disadvantage on all ability checks.
71-75	The creature does whatever anyone tells it to do that isn't obviously self-destructive.
76-80	The creature experiences an overpowering urge to eat something strange, such as dirt, offal, or slime.
81-90	The creature is stunned.
91-00	The creature falls unconscious.

The target can repeat the saving throw at the end of each of its turns. A successful save ends the effect and renders the target immune to the same barrow wight's insanity gaze for 24 hours.

A creature that isn't surprised can avert its eyes to avoid the saving throw at the start of its turn. If the creature does so, it can't see the barrow wight until the start of its next turn, when it can avert its eyes again. If the creature looks at the barrow wight in the meantime, it must immediately make the save.

Resurrection Vulnerability. Casting a *raise dead* or *resurrection* spell on the barrow wight destroys it unless it makes a Wisdom saving throw.

Sunlight Sensitivity. While in sunlight, the barrow wight has disadvantage on attack rolls, as well as on Wisdom (Perception) checks that rely on sight.

ACTIONS

***Slam** Melee weapon attack:* +5 to hit, reach 5 ft., one creature. *Hit:* 6 (1d6+3) bludgeoning damage plus 6 (1d6 + 3) necrotic damage. The target must succeed on a DC 13 Constitution saving throw or its hit point maximum is reduced by an amount equal to the necrotic damage taken. This reduction lasts until the target takes a long rest. The target dies if this effect reduces their hit point maximum to zero.

A humanoid slain by this attack rises 1d4 rounds later as a barrow wight under the control of the wight that killed it, unless the humanoid is restored to life or its body is destroyed. The wight can have no more than three barrow wights under its control at one time.

BLACK BULETTE

Huge monstrosity, lawful evil

Armor Class: 19 (natural armor)
Hit Points: 225 (18d12 + 108)
Speed: 80 ft., burrow 80 ft.

STR	DEX	CON	INT	WIS	CHA
22 (+6)	14 (+2)	22 (+6)	6 (−2)	14 (+2)	10 (+0)

Saving Throws Dex +7, Wis + 7
Skills Perception +7
Damage Immunities fire
Senses blindsight 60 ft., darkvision 60 ft., passive Perception 17
Languages all, telepathy 120 ft.
Challenge 13 (10,000 XP)

Deal of a Lifetime. If killed, the body of a black bulette shatters into shards of obsidian glass, freeing the devil imprisoned within. The devil may be of any random type (GM's discretion) save that of a royal rank. The devil will be grateful to whoever is responsible for ending its centuries-long confinement, and will offer the responsible parties one favor in payment before returning to the infernal realms of its home plane. Wise recipients of this offer should bear in mind that the usual caveats of treating with devils remain in full force when striking any bargains.

Detect Evil and Good. The bulette knows if there is an aberration, celestial, elemental, fey, fiend, or undead within 30 feet of it and where the creature is located. The bulette also knows if there is a place or object within 30 feet of it that has been consecrated or desecrated.

Dual Planar Connection. The black bulette has a planar tie to the Abyss, where it appears as a chained adamantine cask shaped like an abstracted bulette.

Infernal Stench. Any creature that starts its turn within 120 feet of the bulette must succeed on a DC 18 Constitution saving throw or be poisoned until the start of its next turn. Coming into physical contact with a black bulette results in the creature being imparted with a horrid stench that causes it to have disadvantage on Dexterity (Stealth) checks for 12 hours. The stench can be removed sooner with plenty of soap, water, and two full hours of scrubbing.

Magic Resistance. The bulette has advantage on saving throws against spells and other magical effects.

ACTIONS

***Bite.** Melee Weapon Attack:* +11 to hit, reach 10 ft., one target. *Hit:* 58 (8d12 + 6) piercing damage.

Abysmal Breath (recharge 5–6). The bulette exhales fire in a 60-foot cone. Each creature in that area must make a DC 18 Dexterity saving throw, taking 42 (12d6) fire damage on a failed save, or half as much damage on a successful one.

BLACK SKELETON

Medium undead, chaotic evil

Armor Class 17 (chain shirt)
Hit Points 71 (13d8 + 13)
Speed 40 ft.

STR	DEX	CON	INT	WIS	CHA
11 (+0)	19 (+4)	13 (+1)	13 (+1)	10 (+0)	14 (+2)

Skills Perception +4, Stealth +6
Damage Vulnerabilities bludgeoning, radiant
Damage Resistances cold
Damage Immunities necrotic, poison
Condition Immunities exhaustion, poisoned
Senses darkvision 60 ft., passive Perception 14
Languages understands the languages it knew in life but can't speak
Challenge 4 (1,100 XP)

Shortsword Masters. Black skeletons gain defensive bonuses (+2 to AC) and bonuses to attack (+2 to hit) when wielding dual shortswords (included in the statistics).

ACTIONS

Multiattack. The black skeleton makes two claw attacks or two shortsword attacks.
Claw. *Melee Weapon Attack:* +6 to hit, reach 5 ft., one target. *Hit:* 8 (1d8 + 4) slashing damage, and the target's Strength score is reduced by 1d4. The target dies if this reduces its strength to 0. Otherwise, the reduction lasts until the target finishes a short or long rest.
Shortsword. *Melee Weapon Attack:* +8 to hit, reach 5 ft., one target. *Hit:* 11 (2d6 + 4) piercing damage, and the target's Strength score is reduced by 1d4. The target dies if this reduces its strength to 0. Otherwise, the reduction lasts until the target finishes a short or long rest

BONE COBBLER

Medium humanoid, chaotic evil

Armor Class 14 (natural armor)
Hit Points 45 (6d8 + 18)
Speed 30 ft.

STR	DEX	CON	INT	WIS	CHA
14 (+2)	12 (+1)	16 (+3)	10 (+0)	14 (+2)	9 (-1)

Senses darkvision 60 ft., passive Perception 12
Languages Common
Challenge 1/4 (50 XP)

Flesh stripper. A bone cobbler can rapidly strip all the flesh from a human-sized creature in 3 rounds using its claws and hammers. Once stripped, the bone cobbler devours the flesh and collects the victim's bones to use in its "sculptures". A creature slain in this manner can only be brought back to life by a *wish* spell.

ACTIONS

Multiattack. The bone cobbler makes two claw attacks or two hammer attacks.
Claw. *Melee Weapon Attack:* +4 to hit, reach 5 ft., one target. *Hit:* 3 (1d3 + 2) slashing damage.
Hammer. *Melee Weapon Attack:* +4 to hit, reach 5 ft., one target. *Hit:* 5 (1d6 + 2) bludgeoning damage.
Animate Bones (1/day). The bone cobbler animates up to five skeletal statues within 30 feet of itself. The statues fight as **skeletons** and go on their own initiative. The bone cobbler can issue simple instructions to the statues as a free action and the statues follow the instructions to the best of their ability.
The Vapors (recharge 4–6). A bone cobbler bellows forth a cloud of vapors that covers a 10-foot-radius area centered on itself. Each creature in the area other than a bone cobbler must make a DC 13 Constitution saving throw. A creature that fails is slowed for one minute. While slowed, the creature's speed is halved, it has a –2 penalty to armor class and Dexterity saving throws, and it can't use reactions. A creature may repeat the saving throw at the end of each of its turns, ending the effect on a success.

BONE GATE

Large construct, chaotic evil

Armor Class 18 (natural armor)
Hit Points 165 (22d10 + 44)
Speed 0 ft.

STR	DEX	CON	INT	WIS	CHA
24 (+7)	1 (–5)	14 (+2)	8 (–1)	16 (+3)	14 (+2)

Saving Throws Str +11, Con +6, Wis +7, Cha +6
Skills Perception +7
Damage Resistances acid, cold
Damage Immunities fire, lightning, poison; bludgeoning, piercing, and slashing damage from nonmagical attacks
Condition Immunities poisoned, prone
Senses darkvision 600 ft., passive Perception 17
Languages —
Challenge 9 (5,000 XP)

Life Magnet. A creature that is neither an undead nor a construct that hits the bone gate with a melee attack from within 10 feet must succeed on a DC 18 Dexterity saving throw or be grappled by the bone gate (escape DC 18). Until this grapple ends, the target is restrained. At the start of each of the bone gate's turns, the target takes 11 (2d10) necrotic damage. A creature brought to 0 hit points in this way is permanently absorbed into the gate and can't be brought back to life.

Magic Resistance. The bone gate has advantage on saving throws against spells and other magical effects.
Magic Weapons. The bone gate's weapon attacks are magical.
Rejuvenation. If a demon gate is destroyed, it gains a new body in 24 hours, regaining all its hit points and becoming active again.

ACTIONS

Strike. *Melee Weapon Attack:* +11 to hit, reach 10 ft., one target. *Hit:* 29 (4d10 + 7) bludgeoning damage and the target is grappled (escape DC 18). Until this grapple ends, the target is restrained. At the start of each of the bone gate's turns, the target takes 11 (2d10) necrotic damage. A creature brought to 0 hit points in this way is permanently absorbed into the gate and can't be brought back to life.
Tongue. *Melee Weapon Attack:* +14 to hit, reach 15 ft., one target. *Hit:* 26 (4d8 + 8) slashing damage plus 14 (4d6) fire damage.

Brain Rat

Tiny beast, unaligned

Armor Class 10
Hit Points 3 (2d4 − 2)
Speed 20ft., climb 20 ft.

STR	DEX	CON	INT	WIS	CHA
2 (−4)	11 (+0)	9 (−1)	16 (+3)	10 (+0)	8 (−1)

Skills Stealth +2
Senses darkvision 30 ft., passive Perception 10
Languages —
Challenge 1/8 (25 XP)

Innate Spellcasting. The brain rat's innate spellcasting ability is Intelligence (spell save DC 13). It can cast the following spells, requiring no material components.
At will: *detect thoughts*
1/day each: *confusion, feeble mind*
Keen Smell. The rat has advantage on Wisdom (Perception) checks that rely on smell.

Actions

Bite. *Melee Weapon Attack*: +0 to hit, reach 5 ft., one target. *Hit*: 1 piercing damage.
Mind Thrust (3/day). One creature within 30 feet of the brain rat must make a DC 13 Intelligence saving throw. On a failure, it takes 10 (3d6) psychic damage.

Charonademon

Medium fiend (demon), neutral evil

Armor Class 16 (natural armor)
Hit Points 75 (10d8 + 30)
Speed 40 ft.

STR	DEX	CON	INT	WIS	CHA
18 (+4)	16 (+3)	16 (+3)	15 (+2)	14 (+2)	18 (+4)

Saving Throws Con +6, Wis +5
Skills Arcana +6, Deception +8, Intimidation +8, Perception +6, Stealth +7, Survival +6
Damage Resistances cold, fire, lightning; bludgeoning, piercing, and slashing from nonmagical attacks
Damage Immunities acid, poison
Condition Immunities poisoned
Senses darkvision 60 ft., passive Perception 16
Languages Abyssal, Common, Daemonic, Infernal, telepathy 120 ft.
Challenge 7 (2,900 XP)

Innate Spellcasting. The charonademon's innate spellcasting ability is Charisma (spell save DC 16). It can cast the following spells, requiring no material components.
At will: *detect magic, darkness, see invisibility*
1/day: *plane shift* (skiff and self only)
Magic Resistance. The charonademon has advantage on saving throws against spells and other magical effects.
Magic Weapons. The charonademon's weapon attacks are considered magical for the purposes of damage resistances.

Actions

Multiattack. The charonademon uses its Fear Gaze and makes two Quarterstaff attacks.
Quarterstaff. *Melee Weapon Attack:* +7 to hit, reach 5 ft., one target. *Hit*: 11 (2d6 + 4) bludgeoning damage, or 13 (2d8 + 4) bludgeoning damage if used with two hands to make a melee attack.
Fear Gaze. Creatures within 30 feet of the charonademon who can see it must make a DC 16 Wisdom saving throw. On a failed saving throw, the creature takes 10 (3d6) psychic damage and is frightened for 1 minute. On a successful saving throw, the creature takes half damage and is not frightened.
While frightened, the target must take the Dash action and move away from the charonademon by the safest available route on each of its turns, unless there is nowhere to move. The creature can repeat the saving throw if it ends its turn out of line of sight with the charonademon, ending the effect on a success. If the creature's saving throw succeeds, or the effect ends for it, the target is immune to a charonademon's fear gaze for 24 hours.
Summon (1/day). The charonademon has a 35% chance to summon 1d4 **hydrodemons1** or 1 **charonademon1**. The summoned demon appears in an unoccupied space within 60 feet of the charonademon, but can't summon other demons. It remains for 1 minute, until it or the first charonademon is slain, or until the first charonademon takes an action to dismiss it.

Demonic Knight

Medium fiend (demon), chaotic evil

Armor Class 17 (half plate)
Hit Points 85 (10d8 + 40)
Speed 30 ft.

STR	DEX	CON	INT	WIS	CHA
20 (+5)	13 (+1)	18 (+4)	17 (+3)	18 (+4)	18 (+4)

Skills Arcana +6, Athletics +8, Perception +7, Stealth +4
Damage Resistances acid, cold, fire; bludgeoning, piercing, and slashing damage from nonmagical weapons
Condition Immunities charmed, frightened
Senses truesight 60 ft., passive Perception 17
Languages Abyssal, Common
Challenge 6 (2,300 XP)

Innate Spellcasting. The demonic knight's innate spellcasting ability is Charisma (spell save DC 15, +7 to hit with spell attacks). It can cast the following spells without requiring material components:

At will: *detect magic, wall of ice*
2/day: *dispel magic*
1/day each: *bestow curse, fireball*

Magic Weapon. The demonic knight's weapon attacks are considered magical for the purposes of damage resistance.

Actions

Multiattack. The demonic knight makes two longsword attacks, or one one-handed longsword attack and one mailed fist attack.

Longsword. *Melee Weapon Attack:* +8 to hit, reach 5 ft., one target. *Hit:* 9 (1d8 + 5) slashing damage, or 10 (1d10 + 5) slashing damage if used with two hands.

Mailed Fist. *Melee Weapon Attack:* +8 to hit, reach 5 ft., one target. *Hit:* 9 (1d8 + 5) bludgeoning damage.

Breath of Unlife (recharge 5–6). The demonic knight releases a 10-foot cone of necrotic breath. Creatures in the area must make a DC 15 Constitution saving throw. On a failed save, a creature takes 28 (8d6) necrotic damage. If a humanoid creature is slain by this damage, it rises as a shadow demon under the command of the demonic knight that created it. The new shadow demon remains enslaved to the demonic knight until the knight's death and cannot summon demons of its own. A demonic knight can only have two such shadow demons under its command.

Summon Demon (1/day). A demonic knight has a 50 percent chance of summoning 1d4 shadow demons, 2 hezrous, 1 glabrezu, 1 vrock, or 1 marilith. The summoned demon appears in an unoccupied space within 60 feet. It cannot summon further demons and remains only for 1 minute before vanishing. It disappears early if it or the demonic knight is slain.

Emeritus Chaplain

Medium humanoid (any race), any alignment

Armor Class 17 (breastplate, shield)
Hit Points 135 (18d8 + 54)
Speed 30 ft.

STR	DEX	CON	INT	WIS	CHA
18 (+4)	12 (+1)	16 (+3)	14 (+2)	21 (+5)	15 (+2)

Saving Throws Con +7, Wis +9, Cha +6
Skills History +6, Insight +9, Medicine +9, Religion +6
Senses passive Perception 15
Languages any four languages
Challenge 12 (8,400 XP)

Aura of Mettle. At the start of each of the emeritus chaplain's turns, each ally within 10 feet of it, including the emeritus chaplain, that has less than half its maximum hit points regains 5 (2d4) hit points. In addition, each ally within 10 feet of the emeritus chaplain has advantage on saving throws against effects that cause the charmed or frightened conditions.

Divine Weapons. The emeritus chaplain's weapon attacks are magical. When the emeritus chaplain hits with any weapon, the weapon deals an extra 4d8 radiant (good or neutral chaplains) or necrotic (evil chaplains) damage.

Spellcasting. The emeritus chaplain is a 10th-level spellcaster. Its spellcasting ability is Wisdom (spell save DC 17, +9 to hit with spell attacks). The emeritus chaplain has the following cleric spells prepared:

Cantrips (at will): *guidance, light, resistance, sacred flame, thaumaturgy*
1st level (4 slots): *bless, detect evil and good, cure wounds, healing word, inflict wounds*
2nd level (3 slots): *aid, silence, spiritual weapon*
3rd level (3 slots): *dispel magic, mass healing word, spirit guardians*
4th level (3 slots): *freedom of movement, guardian of faith*
5th level (2 slots): *dispel evil and good, mass cure wounds*

Actions

Multiattack. The emeritus chaplain makes three Shortsword attacks.

Shortsword. *Melee Weapon Attack:* +8 to hit, reach 5 ft., one target. *Hit:* 7 (1d6 + 4) piercing damage plus 18 (4d8) radiant (good or neutral chaplains) or necrotic (evil chaplains) damage.

Fallen Paladin

Medium humanoid (any), any evil alignment

Armor Class 20 (plate armor, shield)
Hit Points 100 (12d8 + 24)
Speed 30 ft.

STR	DEX	CON	INT	WIS	CHA
18 (+4)	12 (+1)	14 (+2)	12 (+1)	16 (+3)	18 (+4)

Saving Throws Wis +6, Cha +7
Skills Athletics +7, Medicine +4, Persuasion +7, Religion +4
Senses passive Perception 13
Languages Common, plus one other language
Challenge 8 (3,900 XP)

Unholy Smite. When the fallen paladin hits with a melee weapon attack, it can expend a spell slot to deal additional necrotic damage to the target, in addition to the weapon's damage. The extra damage is 9 (2d8) for a 1st-level spell slot, plus 4 (1d8) for each spell level higher than 1st, to a maximum of 21 (5d8). The damage increases by 4 (1d8) if the target is a celestial.

Unholy Resilience. The fallen paladin is immune to disease, and cannot be charmed or frightened. It has a +4 bonus to any saving throw it makes. These benefits cease to function if the fallen paladin is unconscious or slain.

Spellcasting. The fallen paladin is a 12th-level spellcaster. Its spellcasting ability is Charisma (spell save DC 15). It has the following paladin spells prepared.

1st level (4 slots): *bane, divine favor, protection from evil and good, sanctuary, shield of faith*
2nd level (3 slots): *aid, lesser restoration, hold person, silence*
3rd level (3 slots): *bestow curse, dispel magic, protection from energy*

Actions

Multiattack. The fallen paladin makes two Longsword attacks.

Longsword. *Melee Weapon Attack:* +7 to hit, reach 5 ft., one target. *Hit:* 8 (1d8 + 4) slashing damage, or 9 (1d10 + 4) slashing damage if wielded with two hands, plus 4 (1d8) necrotic damage.

Lay of Hands. The fallen paladin has a pool of 60 hit points to use with its Lay on Hands ability. It regains spent hit points from this pool when it takes a long rest. It can use this ability to cause a creature within 5 feet of it or itself to regain any number of hit points, up to its hit point maximum or the fallen paladin's pool of hit points is reduced to 0.

Unholy Weapon (1/short or long rest). The fallen paladin adds +4 to its attack and damage rolls for 1 minute, and its weapon is considered magical for the purposes of damage resistances.

Fear Guard

Medium undead, chaotic evil

Armor Class 13
Hit Points 58 (9d8 + 18)
Speed fly 30 ft.

STR	DEX	CON	INT	WIS	CHA
6 (–2)	15 (+2)	15 (+2)	10 (+0)	12 (+1)	18 (+4)

Saving Throws Con +2, Wis +3
Skills Acrobatics +6, Insight +5, Perception +5, Stealth +6
Damage Vulnerabilities radiant
Damage Resistances acid, cold, fire, lightning, thunder; bludgeoning, piercing, and slashing from nonmagical attacks
Damage Immunities necrotic, poison
Condition Immunities charmed, exhaustion, grappled, paralyzed, petrified, poisoned, prone, restrained, unconscious
Senses darkvision 60 ft., passive Perception 15
Languages understands all languages it knew in life but can't speak
Challenge 4 (1,100 XP)

Create Spawn. Any living creature reduced to Wisdom 0 by a fear guard is slain and becomes a fear guard under the control of its killer in 1d6 rounds.

Sunlight Sensitivity. A fear guard exposed to natural sunlight suffers 7 (2d6) radiant damage per round of exposure and moves at half its normal speed.

Innate Spellcasting. The fear guard's spellcasting ability is Charisma (spell save DC 14). The fear guard can innately cast the following spells, requiring only verbal components:
At will: *darkness, ray of enfeeblement*

Actions

Incorporeal Touch. *Melee Weapon Attack:* +4 to hit, reach 5 ft., one target. *Hit:* 7 (2d4 + 2) slashing damage and the target loses two points of Wisdom until after it completes a long rest. A creature brought to 0 Wisdom by this attack dies.

Ghoul Lord

Medium undead, chaotic evil

Armor Class 14 (natural armor)
Hit Points 91 (14d8 + 28)
Speed 30 ft.

STR	DEX	CON	INT	WIS	CHA
15 (+2)	16 (+3)	14 (+2)	10 (+0)	16 (+3)	14 (+2)

Damage Immunities necrotic, poison
Condition Immunities paralyzed, poisoned
Senses darkvision, passive Perception 13
Languages Common
Challenge 2 (450 XP)

Spellcasting. The ghoul lord is a 10th-level spellcaster. Its spellcasting ability is Wisdom (spell save DC 13, +5 to hit with spell attacks). It has the following cleric spells prepared:

Cantrips (at will): *acid splash, guidance, sacred flame, thaumaturgy*
1st level (4 slots): *bane, detect magic, inflict wounds*
2nd level (3 slots): *blindness/deafness, hold person, silence, spiritual weapon*
3rd level (3 slots): *bestow curse, clairvoyance, dispel magic, spirit guardians*
4th level (3 slots): *blight, locate creature*
5th level (2 slots): *contagion, dispel evil and good, insect plague*

Turning Defiance. The ghoul lord and any ghouls within 30 feet of it have advantage on saving throws against effects that turn undead.

Actions

Multiattack. The ghoul lord makes two melee attacks.
Claw. Melee Weapon Attack: +5 to hit, reach 5 ft., one target. Hit: 5 (1d6 + 3) slashing damage. If the target is a creature other than an elf or undead, it must succeed on a DC 13 Constitution saving throw or be paralyzed for 1 minute. The target can repeat the saving throw at the end of each of its turns, ending the effect on itself on a success.
Mace. Melee Weapon Attack: +4 to hit, reach 5 ft., one target. Hit: 5 (1d6 + 2) bludgeoning damage.

Ghoulish Giant Rat

Small undead, unaligned

Armor Class (12)
Hit Points 7 (2d6)
Speed 30 ft.

STR	DEX	CON	INT	WIS	CHA
9 (−1)	15 (+2)	11 (+0)	2 (−4)	10 (+0)	4 (−3)

Senses darkvision 60 ft., passive Perception 10
Languages —
Challenge 1/8 (25 XP)

Keen Smell. The ghoulish giant rat has advantage on Wisdom (Perception) checks that rely on smell.
Pack Tactics. The ghoulish giant rat has advantage on an attack roll against a target if at least one of the ghoulish giant rat's allies is within 5 feet of the ghoulish giant rat and the ally isn't incapacitated.

Actions

Bite. Melee Weapon Attack: +4 to hit, reach 5 ft., one target. Hit: 7 (2d4 + 2) piercing damage. If the target is a creature other than an elf or undead, it must succeed on a DC 10 Constitution saving throw or be paralyzed for 1 minute. The target can repeat the saving throw at the end of each of its turns, ending the effect on itself on a success.

Holy Knight

Medium humanoid (any), any alignment

Armor Class 20 (plate, shield)
Hit Points 65 (10d8 + 20)
Speed 30 ft.

STR	DEX	CON	INT	WIS	CHA
16 (+3)	11 (+0)	14 (+2)	11 (+0)	11 (+0)	15 (+2)

Saving Throws Wis +2, Cha +4
Skills Insight +2, Religion +2
Senses passive Perception 10
Languages Common, plus one other language
Challenge 4 (1,100 XP)

Divine Blessings. The holy knight has advantage on saving throws against being frightened, and is immune to disease.
Divine Smite. When the holy knight hits with a melee weapon attack, it can expend a spell slot to deal additional radiant damage to the target, in addition to the weapon's damage. The extra damage is 9 (2d8) for a 1st-level spell slot, plus 4 (1d8) for each spell level higher than 1st, to a maximum of 21 (5d8). The damage increases by 4 (1d8) if the target is a fiend or undead.
Spellcasting. The holy knight is a 5th-level spellcaster. Its spellcasting ability is Charisma (spell save DC 12). It has the following paladin spells.
1st level (4 slots): *bless, divine favor, protection from evil and good, sanctuary, shield of faith*
2nd level (2 slots): *aid, lesser restoration, protection from poison, zone of truth*

Actions

Multiattack. The holy knight makes two Longsword attacks.
Longsword. Melee Weapon Attack: +5 to hit, reach 5 ft., one target. Hit: 7 (1d8 + 3) slashing damage, or 8 (1d10 + 3) slashing damage if used with two hands to make a melee attack.
Lay on Hands. The holy knight has a pool of 25 hit points to use with its Lay on Hands ability. It regains spent hit points from this pool when it takes a long rest. It can use this ability to cause a creature within 5 feet of it or itself to regain any number of hit points, up to its hit point maximum or its pool of hit points is reduced to 0.

Hukeesh the Necromancer

Medium humanoid (any), any alignment

Armor Class 13 (16 with *mage armor*)
Hit Points 32 (5d8 + 10)
Speed 30 ft.

STR	DEX	CON	INT	WIS	CHA
10 (+0)	16 (+3)	14 (+2)	19 (+4)	15 (+2)	11 (+0)

Saving Throws Int +7, Wis +5
Skills Arcana +7, History +7
Senses passive Perception 12
Languages Common
Challenge 5 (1,800 XP)

Spellcasting. Hukeesh is a 6th level spellcaster. His spellcasting ability is Intelligence (spell save DC 14, +6 to hit with spell attacks). He has the following spells prepared:
Cantrips (at will): *acid splash, chill touch, mage hand, poison spray*
1st level (4 slots): *burning hands, false life, mage armor, ray of sickness*
2nd level (3 slots): *blindness/deafness, gentle repose, ray of enfeeblement*
3rd level (3 slots): *animate dead, bestow curse, vampiric touch*

Actions

Dagger. Melee Weapon Attack: +6 to hit, reach 5 ft., one target. Hit: 5 (1d4 + 3) piercing damage.
Sling. Ranged Weapon Attack: +6 to hit, range 30/120 ft., one target. Hit: 5 (1d4 + 3) bludgeoning damage.

Juju Zombie

Medium undead, neutral evil

Armor Class 16 (chain mail)
Hit Points 39 (6d8 + 12)
Speed 30 ft.

STR	DEX	CON	INT	WIS	CHA
20 (+5)	16 (+3)	15 (+2)	4 (−3)	10 (+0)	14 (+2)

Skills Acrobatics +7, Athletics +9
Damage Resistances fire
Damage Immunities cold, lightning, poison
Condition Immunities exhaustion, poisoned
Senses darkvision 60 ft., passive Perception 10
Languages understands the languages it knew in life but can't speak
Challenge 3 (700 XP)

Magic Resistance. The juju zombie has advantage on saving throws against spells and other magical effects.

Turn Resistance. The juju zombie has advantage on saving throws against any effect that turns undead.

Undead Fortitude. If damage reduces the juju zombie to 0 hit points, it must make a Constitution saving throw with a DC of 5 + the damage taken, unless the damage is radiant or from a critical hit. On a success, the zombie drops to 1 hit point instead.

Actions

Multiattack. The juju zombie makes two attacks with its longsword, or one attack with its longsword and one slam attack.

Longsword. *Melee Weapon Attack:* +7 to hit, reach 5 ft., one target. *Hit:* 9 (1d8 + 5) slashing damage, or 10 (1d10 + 5) slashing damage if used with two hands.

Slam. *Melee Weapon Attack:* +7 to hit, reach 5 ft., one target. *Hit:* 12 (2d6 +5) bludgeoning damage.

Skeleton Warrior

Medium undead, neutral evil

Armor Class 19 (+1 plate armor)
Hit Points 97 (13d8 + 39)
Speed 30 ft.

STR	DEX	CON	INT	WIS	CHA
20 (+5)	13 (+1)	16 (+3)	10 (+0)	13 (+1)	14 (+2)

Saving Throws Con +8, Wis +6, Cha +7
Skills Insight +6, Intimidate +7, Perception +6
Damage Resistances piercing and slashing damage from nonmagical attacks
Damage Immunities necrotic, poison
Condition Immunities exhaustion, frightened, poisoned, unconscious
Senses Truesight 60 ft., passive Perception 16
Languages Common, any other language the warrior knew in life
Challenge 14 (11,500 XP)

Legendary Resistance (3/day). If the skeleton warrior fails a saving throw, it can choose to succeed instead.

Track Circlet. A skeleton warrior can track and find its circlet unerringly. It can also find the last person who possessed the circlet.

Unholy Fortitude. Skeleton Warriors have advantage on saving throws against being turned.

Actions

Multiattack. A skeleton warrior makes two Greatsword attacks

+1 Greatsword. *Melee Weapon Attack:* +12 to hit, reach 5 ft., one creature. *Hit:* 14 (2d6 + 7) slashing damage plus 3 (1d6) necrotic damage.

Longbow. *Ranged Weapon Attack:* +6 to hit, range 150 ft./600 ft., one creature. *Hit:* 7 (1d12 + 1) piercing damage plus 7 (2d6) necrotic damage, and the target must make a successful DC 16 Constitution saving throw or be infected with crypt fatigue

Legendary Actions

The skeleton warrior can take up to three legendary actions per round. Legendary actions are taken at the end of another creature's turn, and only one can be taken after each turn.

Attack. The skeleton warrior makes a Greatsword or Longbow attack.

Drain Life. *Melee Weapon Attack:* +10 to hit, reach 5 ft.; one creature. *Hit:* the target must make a successful DC 16 Constitution saving throw or be infected with crypt fatigue. If already infected, a failed saving throw causes the creature to gain another level of exhaustion.

Instill Dread. One living creature within 50 feet of the skeleton warrior, which the skeleton warrior can see, must make a successful DC 15 Wisdom saving throw or be frightened for 2d4 rounds. A successful save renders the target immune to this skeleton warrior's dread for 24 hours.

CRYPT FATIGUE

A creature infected with crypt fatigue gains one level of exhaustion immediately, and gains one more level every time it fails the DC 16 Constitution saving throw after taking damage from a skeleton warrior's longbow. An infected creature must make another DC 16 Constitution saving throw at the end of every long rest; with a successful save, it recovers one level of exhaustion, but with a failed save, it gains one level of exhaustion. The disease is cured when the victim no longer has any levels of exhaustion.

SKELETON WARRIOR'S CIRCLET

In the process of transforming into a skeleton warrior, the dying warrior's soul is trapped in a golden circlet. Anyone possessing one of these circlets can exert control over the skeleton warrior whose soul the circlet contains. To establish control, the controller must be within 300 feet of the skeleton warrior, must wear the circlet, and must spend one full round doing nothing but concentrating on the skeleton warrior. If the controller is not interrupted during this time, resolve a Charisma (Intimidation) contest between the skeleton warrior and the creature with the circlet (note that the skeleton warrior adds its proficiency bonus to Intimidation skill checks). If the wearer of the circlet wins the contest, the skeleton warrior is charmed, views that character as an ally, and interprets any of the character's suggestions in the most positive light. It is not dominated or controlled, but it doesn't feel the urge to immediately kill the wearer of the circlet and recover its soul, either. It would like its soul back eventually, but it can wait until its new ally is slain by some other creature or dies naturally. If the skeleton warrior wins the contest, it is immune from attempts to use the circlet to charm it for 24 hours.

While within 300 feet of the charmed skeleton warrior, a person wearing the circlet can exert the following types of influence over the skeleton warrior. He or she can:

- choose to see through the skeleton warrior's eyes
- try to force the skeleton warrior to attack something by making a successful DC 15 Charisma check (failing the check means the skeleton warrior acts as it chooses)
- try to force the skeleton warrior to take some other action — search an area, move across a room, etc. — by making a successful DC 10 Charisma check (failing the check means the skeleton warrior acts as it chooses);
- try to place the skeleton warrior in "inert mode" by making a successful DC 15 Charisma check. If this check succeeds, the skeleton warrior stands motionless, effectively unconscious and paralyzed, until the wearer of the circlet wills it back into wakefulness. If this check fails, the skeletal warrior is no longer charmed.

While forcing the skeleton warrior to do anything, the circlet wearer can't move or take any other action. If the circlet wearer moves more than 300 feet away from the skeleton warrior or removes the circlet from his or her head while the skeleton warrior is active (not inert), the skeleton warrior is no longer charmed. If someone else becomes the circlet's owner, the skeleton warrior knows instantly; if it was charmed, it's not anymore, and if it was inert, it becomes active again.

If a skeleton warrior ever gains control of the circlet containing its soul, it places the circlet on its head and "dies," vanishing in a flash of light. The circlet falls to the ground and crumbles to dust.

SKIN STITCHER

Medium humanoid, chaotic evil

Armor Class 15 (natural armor)
Hit Points 52 (8d8 + 16)
Speed 30 ft.

STR	DEX	CON	INT	WIS	CHA
16 (+3)	12 (+1)	15 (+2)	9 (-1)	12 (+1)	7 (-2)

Skills Athletics +5
Senses darkvision 60 ft., passive Perception 11
Languages Common, Orc
Challenge 1/2 (100 XP)

Savage Attacks. When the skin stitcher scores a critical hit with a melee weapon attack, it can roll one of the weapon's damage dice one additional time and add it to the extra damage of the critical.

ACTIONS

Multiattack. The skin stitcher makes two melee attacks.
Barbed Chains. *Melee Weapon Attack:* +5 to hit, reach 5 ft., one target. *Hit:* 10 (2d6+3) slashing damage.
Claw. *Melee Weapon Attack:* +5 to hit, reach 5 ft., one target. *Hit:* 6 (1d6+3) slashing damage.

ZOMBIE HORDE

Huge swarm of Medium undead, neutral evil

Armor Class 8
Hit Points 127 (15d12 + 36)
Speed 20 ft.

STR	DEX	CON	INT	WIS	CHA
15 (+2)	6 (–2)	16 (+3)	3 (–4)	6 (–2)	5 (–3)

Condition Immunities exhaustion, frightened, poisoned, unconscious
Senses darkvision 60 ft., passive Perception 8
Languages understands all languages they spoke in life but can't speak
Challenge 6 (2,300 XP)

Damage Threshold. If the zombie horde is hit with an attack that does less than 15 hit points of damage, it takes no damage.
Immobilizing Swarm. The swarm can occupy another creature's space and vice versa, and the swarm can move through any opening large enough for a Medium creature. The swarm can't regain hit points or gain temporary hit points. A Large or smaller creature sharing a space with a zombie horde is restrained (escape DC 14). A creature that ends its turn sharing a space with a zombie hoard must make a DC 14 Dexterity saving throw, taking 16 (4d6 + 2) bludgeoning damage on a failure or half as much on a success. If the swarm has half of its hit points or fewer, the damage is 8 (2d6 + 2) bludgeoning damage on a failure and half this amount on a success.
Fetid Aura. A creature that starts its turn within 30 feet of the zombie horde must succeed on a DC 14 Constitution saving throw or become poisoned for one minute. A poisoned creature may repeat the saving throw at the end of each of its turns, ending the effect on a success. A creature for whom the effect has ended is immune to the condition from this horde for 24 hours.

ACTIONS

Slam. *Melee Weapon Attack:* +4 to hit, one creature in the swarm's space. *Hit:* 16 (4d6 + 2) bludgeoning damage, or 8 (2d6 + 2) bludgeoning damage if the swarm has half of its hit points or fewer.

ADVENTURES
WORTH
WINNING